Magic on Robins' Hill

by Diane Marie Krämer

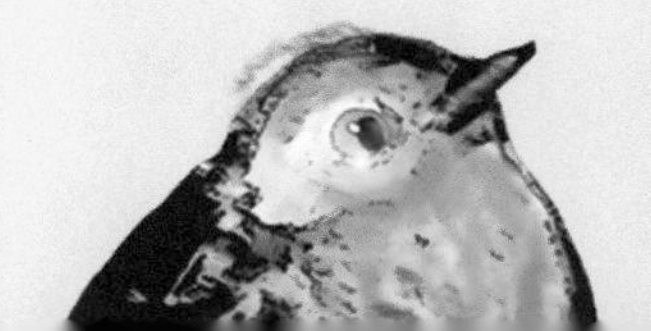

A special thank you to my mom and my husband Michael for
believing and supporting my creative expressions.

FriesenPress

Suite 300 - 990 Fort St
Victoria, BC, V8V 3K2
Canada

www.friesenpress.com

First Edition — 2019

For information contact Diane Marie Krämer: studiokramer@yahoo.com
www.dianemariekramer.com

ISBN
978-1-5255-4655-6 (Hardcover)
978-1-5255-4656-3 (Paperback)
978-1-5255-4657-0 (eBook)

1. JUVENILE FICTION, ANIMALS, BIRDS

Distributed to the trade by The Ingram Book Company

Dedication

This book is written in honor of all my dogs,
family and good friends
departed and living.

May we always embrace
each other with
love and kindness
and always
remember
where we came from.

To always honor those who share
or have shared
our path
our hearts
forever rooted
in love and in wisdom.

A SYMPHONY of Plants, Flowers, and Trees

graciously offering **shelter and home**

to all creatures living

BOTH KNOWN & UNKNOWN.

SPINNING AND TWIRLING

in mid afternoon warm sun.

Dashingly dancing

rainbow colored windmills

YELLOW, GREEN, BLUE,

PURPLE, RED, and ORANGE, too.

All are **one** & all are **well**

Here on Magic Robins' **Hill.**

A STEEP, enchanting, stone

MAGICAL PATH

illuminated by Lanterns

of Cosmic Energies.

Healing Light guiding the WAY

STONE BY STONE

both night and DAY.

The LOG HOUSE on Magic Robins' Hill

stands like no other,

receptive & nurturing

like Sacred Earth Mother.

Silent Protectors stand ever so still

LOYAL FRIENDS to all who live

on Magic Robins' Hill.

Hanging and dangling

from wooden sturdy rafters

SOUNDS

of fluttering

blue bird wings

& all feathered beings

Laughter.

BRIGHTLY DECORATED

Flower Pots

arranged in a non–perfect row

patiently…waiting

for the magical moment

when FLOWERS

WILL GROW!

SCURRYING - SASHAYING

PAWS OF SPEED

a Freeway of chuckling & clattering Chipmunks

DASHING

In between WHIMSICAL 3

To TALL funky woman

& her EVER loving DOG.

A Carnival of Characters and Colors you will find

on the front porch of the house

made from wooden cedar logs.

The red door opens...

The ECCENTRIC ARTIST appears.

RED CLOGS

A-Clunking

BRIGHT SMILE

from ear to ear!

Inquisitive Eyes that follow

– Peeking out from behind the screen door

belonging to

ODIN and Cézanne BLUE.

LOVE, JOY and DEVOTION

truer and true

Best friends ever

Her ODIN and Cézanne BLUE.

In her hand–

the artist with multicolored hair

carries a very PECULIAR

WATERING CAN.

Bending over each clay pot

3 Taps to the CHIME–

3 clucks to the CLOGS–

right on the dot!

Carefully sprinkling
HEALING, PEACE AND LOVE...
Ancestral Magic Stardust
TWINKLING
FROM ABOVE.

The red door closes...

The ROBINS are here!

ABRACADABRA!

Flowers appear!

Invitation

Come on in. The artist with multicolored hair invites you to share a world where generations of robins are the keepers of the land, the protectors of all material and invisible things that live on the Magic Robins' Hill.

Look over here. A front porch filled with enchanted sculptures that are both guardians and citadel for many critters, including the robins who lay their aquamarine marbles within them, giving wing and song to baby robins year in and year out.

Look over there. Colorful windmills and playful wind chimes composing rainbows of song and dance.

Come, experience the magical watering and two dogs with hearts of gold and spirits of fun. It is time to open you hearts and let in the magic on Robins' Hill!

DIANE MARIE KRÄMER

Born January 30th on a Saturday during cartoon hours.

Diane inhabits a world of constant creation. She approaches art with intuition and works in sculpture, photography and painting. She has exhibited her artwork professionally in selected, group and solo shows across the United States and Europe.

Diane is a studio artist and a teaching artist who has many years of experience instructing in different genres in private and public schools, universities and art centers. She has been privileged by having students of all ages and has a special focus on teaching people with disabilities.

Her home is in an enchanted forest in Michigan which she shares with creatures of the wind: the fragile and turbulent robins, chasing grasshoppers, hunting for berries, flooding the trails full of mystery with their symphony of flutes.

Diane lives there with her husband, Michael and her Australian shepherds who bring her great comfort & happiness.

www.dianemariekramer.com
B.A M.A. M.F.A

Artist Testimonials

Diane Marie Krämer is a shaman, whose journeys are reflected in her art and stories. Appreciate the colourful whimsy of her work, but do not be fooled by its seeming simplicity. "Magic on Robins' Hill" is an allegorical tale, expressing Krämer's deep love for humans and other creatures, for family, hearth and home, and our beloved earth. She longs to provide shelter for all, and promises a receptive and nurturing atmosphere to any being fortunate enough to accept her offering. The eccentric artist, with her multicolored hair, describes a place that is magical, indeed. Implicit in her invitation is the belief that if we guard the sacred, we will also experience the powerful and ancient magic she so poetically describes.

Carol Wiebe

PM (Prolific Maker) of her domain • CAWeStruck.com
(in Canada PM stands for Prime Minister)

There is something wonderfully compelling, nay rather intoxicating in the manner Diane Marie Krämer bites into life through her words and visual creations. It is not pure chance that the name Shewolf has clung to her like a hide in a world of Jekylls. Imagine something of an Alice in Wonderland weaponized as Alberto Giacometti and a strong sense of the totemic. Some tiptoe down the rabbit hole, the Shewolf, beautiful inside and out, takes the plunge leaving scratch marks in the form of poetry, statues, three-dimensional paintings and drive-by photographs, that stir the soul; her artistry is not for the faint of heart, although she displays gentleness and humor along with her forays into the primeval. Stick with her, the journey will make you dizzy and the hangover will force you to laugh at the stars.

Michael Kent

Author of "the big Jiggety"
https://www.amazon.com/Michael-Kent/e/B001HCZM1W

Diane Krämer's lively and expressive artwork introduces the critters who frequent her porch and Krämer's sculptures who guard this enchanting world. The poetic language reveals the magic and mystery she uncovers in daily life on Robins' Hill.

Sarah Grusin

retired Smithsonian writer and artist in training.

2019 -

To My Beautiful & Loving Mother -

Thank you for all your hard work, love & Support.... all these years so I can continue to do what I was Born to do!

I love you more then Chocolate!

Love - Diane

xoxoxo

schnukiputz

CPSIA information can be obtained
at www.ICGtesting.com
Printed in the USA
BVHW021340100419
545107BV00005B/23/P